Trek Learns About
TEXTURE

Editorial

Vice President and Editor
in Chief
  Paul A. Kobasa
Associate Manager,
Supplementary Publications
  Cassie Mayer
Manager, Research,
Supplementary Publications
  Cheryl Graham
Manager, Contracts & Compliance
(Rights & Permissions)
  Loranne K. Shields

Graphics and Design

Manager
  Tom Evans
Senior Designer
  Don Di Sante

Production

Director, Manufacturing
and Pre-Press
  Carma Fazio
Manufacturing Manager
  Steven K. Hueppchen
Senior Production Manager
  Janice Rossing
Production/Technology
Manager
  Anne Fritzinger
Proofreader
  Emilie Schrage

World Book, Inc.
233 N. Michigan Ave.
Chicago, IL 60601
U.S.A.

For information about other World Book publications, visit
our Web site at **http://www.worldbookonline.com**
or call **1-800-WORLDBK (967-5325).**

For information about sales to schools and libraries, call
1-800-975-3250 (United States), or **1-800-837-5365 (Canada).**

Trek Learns About Texture
This edition: ISBN 978-0-7166-1916-1

Printed in China by Leo Paper
Products LTD.,
Heshan, Guangdong
1st printing August 2010

Lexile measure: 610

Note to Educators
Activities appear on pages 38-39
of this book. You may make copies
of these pages and distribute them
to students.

Trek Learns About
TEXTURE

Story by Felicia Law
Illustrations by Steve Smallman
and Shirley Tourret

a Scott Fetzer company
Chicago

www.worldbookonline.com

Signora Pittipatti shook the crumbs from the red check tablecloths and straightened the chairs.

Then she went inside the restaurant, and turned the sign to "CLOSED."

Lunchtime was over. The restaurants were all shut. Everyone was indoors resting in the cool.

"Come on," said Crow, "I'm hungry. It's time for our lunch now!"

Behind the restaurant
was a shady yard.
Here Signora Pittipatti
hung the washing.

Here she beat the carpets.

Here she chatted with her neighbors.

9

And it was here that she put out the leftover food from the kitchen to feed the birds.

"What a feast!" said Wagtail excitedly. But Trek stared at the plates of cold food glumly.

"Try a bread roll," said Wagtail, his beak covered in crumbs. "The crust is a bit rough and dry, but you can peck it until it's soft and crumbly."

"Have some pizza," said
Seagull, munching greedily.
"The crust is crisp, but the top
is soft and chewy."

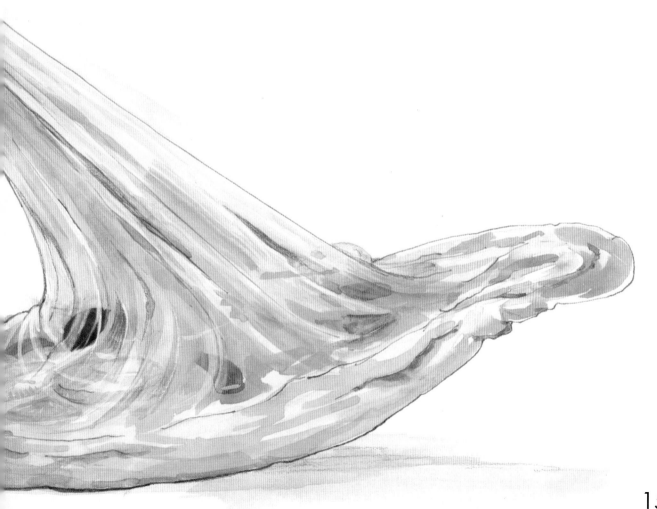

"The spaghetti's excellent," said Crow, tossing slippery strands down his throat as if they were long, wriggly worms.

"Only a woodpecker could eat this cheese," grumbled Seagull. "It's too hard and too dry."

"I much prefer this peach," said Seagull. "It's soft and juicy!"

"Like the grapes," agreed
Wagtail, who really
preferred to eat the hard,
crunchy seeds inside.

Poor Trek. Before he could even try any of the leftover food, the birds had gobbled every last crumb.

Just then, Signora Pittipatti
glanced out of the window.
"Poverino!" she cried, and
threw her hands in the air.
"Those greedy birds have left
nothing for you!"

24

And she hurried to the kitchen to make Trek a huge ice cream.

"There," she said fondly, giving Trek the delicious treat. "Just for you!"

Trek's eyes widened with delight. He dipped the spoon into the huge dish, and slowly licked it clean.

The ice cream was cold—
and smooth—and creamy—
and filled with soft, chewy
cherries and crisp, crunchy
nuts, topped with a mountain
of whipped cream.

Trek looked at his friends over the top of his ice cream. He felt guilty eating it all himself.

   "Would you like some?" he asked.

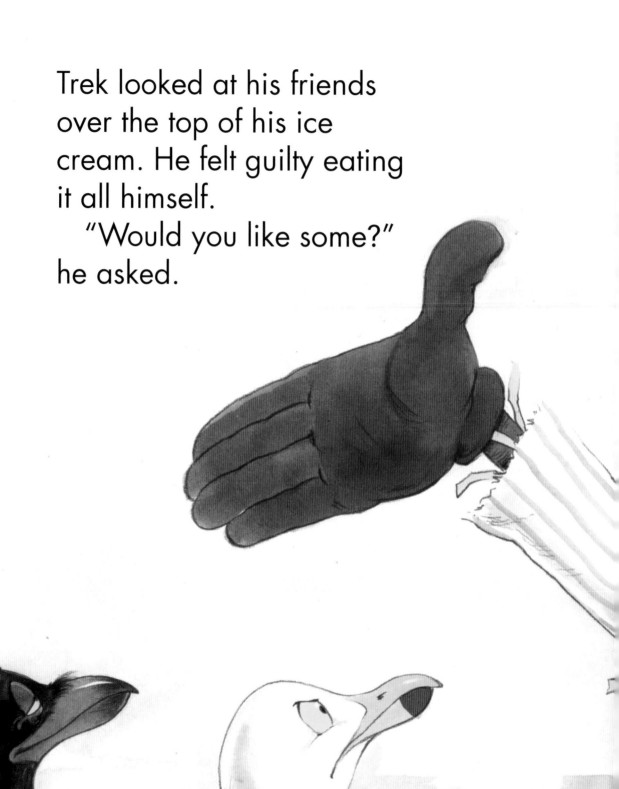

33

But Wagtail said he
would prefer a sip of
cool, fresh water.

Seagull said she never
ate food that was fattening.

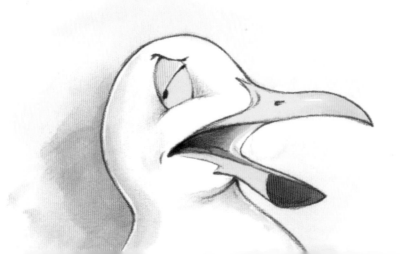

And Crow had already
dozed off for his afternoon
siesta.

Let's feel smooth things.

Let's feel rough things.

Activities

Ask an adult to photocopy these pages so you can complete the activities.

Color the picture using this key.

red = 1   yellow = 2   blue = 3 green = 4

Color the table cloth red and white.

Join the dots and color. You can check your
work against the illustration on page 40.